J. O. Wells

Diary of a Rough Rider

J. O. Wells

Diary of a Rough Rider

ISBN/EAN: 9783337121952

Printed in Europe, USA, Canada, Australia, Japan

Cover: Foto ©Raphael Reischuk / pixelio.de

More available books at **www.hansebooks.com**

Diary of a Rough Rider

J. O. Wells, Harvard, '00.

INTRODUCTION.

WHEN on the evening of April 23rd, 1898, I saw by the Boston papers that the first shot had been fired and that war was inevitable, it was not a question with me whether to enlist or not, but in what branch of the service to enlist; for I had no one dependent upon me and would only throw away my own prospects if I did not return. After a little consideration I decided that I was best fitted for the cavalry. Accordingly when Guy Murchie and Stanley Hollister of the Harvard Law School called on me and asked if I would volunteer to go with a western regiment to be composed of both crack shots and good riders, which was being organized by Dr. Wood and Theodore Roosevelt, both Harvard graduates, I readily assented. Mr. Murchie had authority to recruit ten of the best men in college and as there were a large number who desired to go I feared I had but a small chance; nevertheless Saturday, April 30th, Mr. Murchie advised me that I was to be one of the ten to go and to be ready at a minute's notice. Absolute secrecy was maintained and it was some time before I discovered the identity of the rest of the party; when I did so I found that they were nearly all crack athletes with more or less experience on the big ranches of the west. The party was composed of Guy Murchie, second year law; "Dave" Goodrich, '98; Charles Bull, '98; Stanley Hollister, first year law; Harry Holt, '98; William

Scudder, '99 ; William Saunders, '99 ; Locket Coleman, '99 ; G. H. Scull, '98 ; W. S. Simpson, '99 ; S. K. Gerard and myself.

Monday, May 2nd, Murchie notified me that we were to leave for Washington that night ; accordingly I immediately made the necessary preparation, such as telegraphing home, arranging for leave of absence from college, etc. That night quite a send off was given me in my rooms by classmates and friends. Bidding good-bye to old Cambridge, I caught a Subway car and was soon at the Providence depot where I found the rest of the party with a few friends. We left Boston at 12 p. m. and reached Washington at 2 p. m. the following afternoon, registering at the Shoreham House. Signs of the approaching war were to be seen on every hand. Officers in bright uniforms were to be seen constantly, while artillery now and then rumbled through the peaceful streets. The news of Dewey's victory in the Philippines had just been confirmed and the streets in front of the bulletin boards were crowded.

Wednesday morning we called on Roosevelt at the Navy building and received a most cordial greeting. After a long talk concerning the hardships and work ahead of us, he took us over to the enlisting office on G street where we all successfully passed a very strict physical examination and were sworn into the United States service " for two years unless sooner discharged." We were then placed in charge of Charlie Bull with instructions to report to Colonel Wood at San Antonio, Texas, not later than Monday, May 9th.

We left Washington at 10 p. m. Wednesday evening in a special sleeper provided by ex-Senator Coleman, and reached St. Louis at 7 a. m. Friday. Here we stopped at the Crand Avenue Hotel and were tendered the privileges of the University Club. That evening we were banqueted by the members of the Harvard Club and given a royal send off. On occount of a wash-out we were obliged to leave St. Louis over the Iron Mountain route, and after a hot, dusty, all-day ride Sunday we reached San Antonio Monday noon. Leaving our dress suit cases at the station and rolling our toilet cases, underwear, etc., in our rubber blankets we started for the Menger Hotel where we took leave of civilization in a dollar dinner. After dinner we started for the fair grounds where the camp was located. I shall never forget my first view of the sturdy Westerners when we turned the angle in the woods that warm May afternoon and tramped into the park where Colonel Wood was recruiting his regiment. This park stands near the ruins of two old Indian missions, several miles from town, on the little river which, palm begirdled, worms its way among the quaint adobe houses of San Antonio. The cowboys, hearing the " trolley " beyond the board fence of the park, had lined up in ranks of welcome at the door of the old fair building which served as barracks. As we came in sight through the gate a lusty cheer rose up for the " college boys " and we quickly found ourselves in a hand-gripping mix-up with two hundred strong-wristed troopers, two hundred vigorous personalities in motley pant and suspender, surmounted by alert-eyed coun-tenances which not seldom were decorated without by the quid within, forming, meanwhile, an inter-esting halo to the occasion. In spite of this royal beginning to the new life, it seemed a long and diffi-cult reach from the accustomed pulses of the " college yard " to the wrists of these restive soldiers of the West, keen as on their home plains to monopolize all that the eye could see. Surely here were two planets

indeed, one behind, once lived in and just left, the
other irretrievably entered on for two years, presum-
ably, with no link between except the bundle of
clothes dangling from our backs.   However, we were
given no time to philosophize.   One of the welcomers,
apparently a sort of St. Peter (later discovered to be
no other than "Happy Jack" Hodgkins, with a
pugilistic past), suggested that we be taken down to
the picket line, a few steps below the barracks, to see
the horses.   By the time views as to the prowess of
man and horse in general and the Arizona Rough
Rider in particular had been discussed and agreed to,
evening had come, so Bugler Cassi sounded mess call.
Supper consisted of every one's helping himself to
jacketed potatoes, pushed down in digestive encouragement by a few gulps of coffee, and every one did,
but we from the other planet had had too recent a fill
of civilized food to enjoy with greed the fodder of
Mars doled out by the war department.   When "taps"
sounded we unrolled our rubber blanket on the
barrack-room floor, happy at having been so speedily
assimilated and already asked to join on the morrow
Arizona's proud columns.   When the big plainsmen,
manly and sensitive, found that their rights were not
being tampered with by the "college dandies" and
that we wanted no other office in the regiment than
to fight as troopers beside them, they opened their
hearts to us and in every way kindly fathered their
"mascots."   In this almost comic and most serious
way Harvard sandwiched herself into the intimate
make-up of these first volunteer cavalrymen and
henceforth through the campaign her name played
the synonym for colleges and an approved patriotic
East.

   Of course we are not the only Easterners in the
regiment for Roosevelt has many old friends with

him. However the bulk of the men who make up the regiment and give it its peculiar character come from the four territories which yet remain within the boundaries of the United States; that is from the lands that have been most recently won over to civilization and in which the conditions of life are nearest those that obtained on the frontier when there still was a frontier. They are a splendid set of men, these Southwesterners—tall and sinewy, with resolute, weather beaten faces and eyes that look a man straight in the face without flinching. They include in their ranks men from every occupation, but the three types are those of the cowboy, the hunter and the mining prospector.

In all the world there can be no better material for soldiers than that afforded by these grim hunters of the mountains, these wild rough-riders of the plains. They are accustomed to handling wild and savage horses, they are accustomed to following the chase with the rifle, both for sport and as a means of livelihood. Varied as their occupations are, they have all at one time or another herded cattle and hunted big game. They are hardened to life in the open and to shifting for themselves under adverse circumstances. They are used, for all their lawless freedom, to the rough discipline of the round-up and the mining camp. Some of them are from small frontier towns but most of them are from the wilderness, having left their lonely hunter's cabins and shifting cow-camps to seek new and more stirring adventures beyond the sea. They have their natural leaders—men who have shown they could master other men and could hold their own in the eager, driving life of the new settlements.

Our officers are men who have campaigned in the regular army against the Apache, Ute and Cheyenne, and who on completing their term of service, have shown their energy by settling in new communities and grown up to be men of mark, or they are sheriffs, marshals and deputy marshals—men who have waged relentless war upon the bands of white desperadoes so common in the west.   For example there is Bucky O'Neil of B troop, who is famous throughout the West for his feats of victorious warfare against the Apache and white road agents alike.   He appears to be a born soldier, a born leader of men.   He is a wild, reckless fellow, soft spoken, but of dauntless courage and boundless ambition. Then there is Captain Capron of L troop, who is the perfect ideal of an American soldier—tall and lithe with yellow hair and piercing blue eyes.   He appears the very archtype of the fighting man.

All—officers and soldiers alike, Easterners, Westerners, Northerners and Southerners, cowboys and college graduates, wherever they come from and whatever their social position—possess in common the traits of hardihood and a thirst for adventure. They are to a man, born adventurers, in the old sense of the word.

CHAPTER I.

TUESDAY, MAY 10TH.

I was awakened at four o'clock this morning by reveille and after making a hasty toilet at the hydrant, turned out to mess with D troop from Oklahoma. Being hungry I succeeded in storing away my share of bacon, potatoes and coffee which constituted the breakfast. After breakfast we all reported to Colonel Wood at headquarters. Harry Holt and I then got a pass and went into town where we took a good swim in the natatorium, and after purchasing a few supplies returned to camp feeling much refreshed. We found that during our absence the New Mexico troops and a squad of Eastern troopers had arrived. Among the latter were William Tiffany, Hamilton Fish, Craig Wadsworth and Woodbury Kane, all millionaires and popular society men of New York City. This makes nearly seven hundred men in camp. In the evening the quartermaster issued us half a blanket apiece. After Harry and I got some hay from the stable guard we made a fine bed and rested our bones which still ached from lying on the hard floor the night before. It was pleasant lying on the soft hay to hear the sentinel call the hours, and the regular "all's well" certainly gave a feeling of safety.

WEDNESDAY, MAY 11TH.

After a fine night's rest I arose fresh at reveille and hurriedly dressing in the dim light, ran out and saw the troops answer roll call. After breakfast Colonel Wood sent for us and assigned us to our troops. Simpson, Holt and I are assigned to D troop which is from Oklahoma. We immediately reported to Captain Heuston who commands the troop, and he instructed First Sergeant Palmer to enroll us. Nearly all the troop is composed of young fellows, prospectors, ranchmen and cowboys by vocation. Our captain was formerly colonel in the national guard and is a lawyer by profession as is also our first lieutenant, McGinnes. Our First Sergeant Palmer was formerly a school teacher. We took our blankets over to our new quarters and proceeded to get acquainted with our new-found comrades. Among them is a full-blooded Pawnee Indian, Pollock by name. He is a graduate of three Indian schools and a fine sculptor.

In the afternoon we drilled with D troop on the parade ground and in the woods. Our drill consisted of marching by fours and "deploying as skirmishers." With the mercury at one hundred degrees, we chased all over a new made corn field under the sharp orders of Captain Heuston who is evidently an old hand at the business.

THURSDAY, MAY 12TH.

This morning we had a long "extended order" drill which thoroughly tired us out. In the afternoon Harry and I got a pass and went into town and had another fine swim. We saw a good deal of the city. The old Alamo where Captain Houston and Dave Crockett fought to the death with odds of ten to one against them still stands as a monument to the valor of Americans. The streets in "San Antone," as it is called, are narrow and lined with squalid looking adobe buildings. The inhabitants are mostly of Mexican descent and the women are remarkable for their beauty. The city has a good many open squares or parks called plazas.

FRIDAY, MAY 13TH.

When the details were made out this morning I found that I was on the main guard for twenty-four hours. The guard consists of three reliefs of nine men each, so each man has two hours on and four off. I found that the officer of the guard was Lieutenant Keyes, formerly of the famous Seventh Cavalry, while Bucky O'Neil, captain of B troop, was officer of the day. I was on post No. 5, in front of headquarters. The sun was very hot and there being no shade I suffered intensely. About midnight, just as I had been relieved and was trying to take a little nap, Captain O'Neil called out my relief and marched us down to the street car track to arrest all men returning without passes. We ambushed the car but the motorman refused to stop ; Lieutenant Keyes jumped and caught the car and I followed him ; after the car stopped he commended me for my alertness as the other men failed to get the car. We marched all the men up to the guard house but failed to find any without passes. At two o'clock I went on guard again and when I was relieved at four I was pretty tired.

SATURDAY, MAY 14TH.

I found the sun unbearably hot on my post to-day and was glad when the new guard came on at five in the afternoon. During the day our brown canvas uniforms were issued us and we now begin to look like soldiers. A good many men are getting sick, owing to the wretched drinking water we have. I am training myself to get along on as little water as possible, for in Cuba the water is certain to be bad.

SUNDAY, MAY 15TH.

I was on " old guard fatigue " today and worked hard in the hot sun all the morning cleaning up the grounds for services which were held in the barracks by Chaplain Brown. There have been hundreds of visitors to the grounds all day. In the afternoon I had a slight attack of fever.

MONDAY, MAY 16TH.

Had a bad night, tossed all night on the hard floor with a burning fever and no water. My temperature this morning was 103 degrees. I have been put on the sick list and am off duty today but hope to be able to report tomorrow. The surgeon came in and gave me a few pills, and Burgess, one of the men who used to be a professional nurse, bathed my hands and face with cool water. Some of the other boys divided a fine lunch with me which their lady friends had sent out from town.

TUESDAY, MAY 17TH.

Temperature much lower today so I reported for duty and was put on police duty inside the building, as the fever had left me too weak to drill.

WEDNESDAY, MAY 18TH.

I was issued my saddle, blanket, spurs and bridle today. We had a long drill in the morning and a skirmish drill in the afternoon. Several of the men are so sick that they had to be sent to the hospital today. If we don't leave here soon we will have all the men on the sick list.

THURSDAY, MAY 19TH.

I drew my horse today. My lot number was

forty-three but I drew a very good saddler. He is a strawberry roan weighing about eight hundred pounds and saddle marked. His teeth show him to be about five years old. In the forenoon we had our first mounted drill, lasting four hours. A great many of the horses were very vicious and some of the men were thrown. I found that my horse has an unpleasant habit of kicking whenever he is spurred. The dust on the line of march was something terrible and when we returned we were hardly able to recognize one another. In the afternoon while we were having another skirmish drill dismounted, K troop tried their new rapid firing guns, presented by Woodbury Kane and William Tiffany. These guns can be fired about seven hundred times per minute and are very effective up to fifteen hundred yards.

FRIDAY, MAY 20TH.

To-day we were given our "dog tents" (tents about four feet high, four feet wide and five feet long.) Each tent is occupied by two troopers and when on the march each trooper carries half the tent. Harry and I are to bunk together. I like him very much. At college he was captain of the base ball team and a crack tennis player. His home is in Denver, Colorado. In the evening I attended the concert given in our honor at the beer garden just outside the grounds. There were a good many ladies from the city present and I had a very enjoyable time.

SATURDAY, MAY 21ST.

I came down with the fever again this morning and remained in quarters all day. We received our six shooters and Krag-Jorgensen carbines this morning. The indications are that we will move before long.

SUNDAY, MAY 22ND.

My fever still hangs on, but I reported for duty this morning and was put on horse guard under Sergeant Randolph. During the day the articles of war were read to the regiment, which was kept standing "at attention" in the hot sun for over an hour. About half a dozen men fainted away under the strain.

MONDAY, MAY 23RD.

I passed a rather bad night but reported for duty again to-day and was put on "interior guard." The boys are all very kind to me. They want me to go to the hospital but I prefer to stick it out here.

TUESDAY, MAY 24TH.

We had another four-hour mounted drill this morning. The sun was fearfully hot and the horses suffered a good deal. In the afternoon we had a long skirmish drill. I received a tremendous mail to-day, fourteen letters in all.

WEDNESDAY, MAY 25TH.

My fever was up to 105 degrees this morning and I was sent to the hospital at Fort Sam Houston. Arriving there I received a cooling bath and was then placed in a clean white cot and given some bread and milk. How good it seemed to get in a bed once more.

THURSDAY, MAY 26TH.

My fever increased to 106¼ degrees to-day, but after a nice visit with Harry, who came out to see me, I felt much better. Harry says the regiment will not leave for some time so I will have lots of chance to get well before they leave.

FRIDAY, MAY 27TH.

My temperature has dropped to 95 degrees and I feel much better. . The doctor says I will have to stay in the hospital some time yet. I weighed myself this morning and found that I had lost twenty-five pounds since enlisting.

SATURDAY, MAY 28TH.

Harry Holt came out again to see me and told me I had better follow the surgeon's advice and stay where I am a week or two. He said that the regiment was being drilled into shape very fast and presented a very good appearance now. About dark Johnson came out with my mail, some dozen letters in all, which I read with a good deal of pleasure.

SUNDAY, MAY 29TH.

My fever is 103 degrees today but I feel much stronger. I was surprised to see by the paper this morning that the regiment was to leave for Tampa this morning. I immediately determined to join it, but the major in command of the hospital told me I could not go for two or three weeks as I would need all that time to recuperate in. Having made up my mind, however, I was bound to go. So after the major had left the ward I called my nurse and gave him five dollars to get my clothes for me. As soon as I could get into them I stole out the back way and started for camp. Arriving at camp I found that D troop had gone with the first squadron and I was told that the section had already left for Tampa. Greatly disappointed, I reported to Colonel Roosevelt at headquarters and was assigned to Troop I, under Captain

McGinnis, until we should reach Tampa, as the regiment was travelling in three sections and it would be impossible for me to join my troop until we reached Tampa. Just as I was reporting to Captain McGinnis an orderly dashed up and from him I learned that the first section had been delayed and would not be ready to leave for a full half hour yet. With hopes of catching my troop before they left San Antonio, I hurried to Colonel Roosevelt and got a pass. Leaving the grounds, I took an electric to the railroad crossing and then started down the track, intending to flag the train if it started before I made the three miles to the stock yards where the horses were being loaded. The sun was blazing hot and in my weakened condition I had to often stop and rest. Just as I reached a railroad crossing I heard a whistle and looking ahead I saw the train coming. Knowing that it would slow up at the crossing I sat down and rested. The train soon reached me and as it drew near I saw Sal Newcomb, Beal and Muxlow on the first car, which was a stock car containing our horses. As the train slowed up I jumped and caught it, being heartily welcomed by the boys on top of the car who thought I had been left behind in the hospital. When we reached the station I was a good deal exhausted so I went back into the D troop coach and reported to Captain Heuston, who very kindly relieved me of all duty until we reached Tampa. The boys crowded around me and shook hands as if I had been away on a long journey. Although the men were crowded two in a seat, they immediately fixed up a couple of seats so I could lie down and Muxlow appointed himself my nurse. I was weak from the exertion and soon dropped off to sleep, awakening about noon feeling better than I had for a week and with my fever entirely gone. Some of the boys had

received lunches from their lady friends in San
Antonio, and I was speedily supplied with all the
dainties the lunch boxes contained. We have three
days' rations with us and expect to be on the road
about forty-eight hours.

MONDAY, MAY 30TH.

I awoke feeling much better this morning. Our
first stop was made at Houston, Texas, where we
watered and fed the horses. This delayed us about
six hours. There was an immense crowd at the
depot, and we were given a big send off. All the
afternoon we have been riding through a delightful
country, the air being filled with the fragrance of
magnolia blooms which fairly whiten the trees along
the route. The boys have been passing away the
time holding mock court. Our rations consist of hard
tack and canned corn beef which is very good.
Newcomb and Beal appropriated a chicken at Houston
and made some excellent broth from it which they
insisted on my drinking. I never had anything taste
better or take effect quicker than that chicken broth.

TUESDAY, MAY 31ST.

We reached New Orleans to-day at noon and
were ferried across the river. We were given a very
noisy welcome here, every steam whistle in town was
blown and it seemed as if the entire city had turned
out to greet us. They brought us flowers, they
brought us watermelons and other fruits, and sometimes jugs and pails of milk, all of which we much
appreciated. We have been traveling through a
region where practically all the older men have served
in the Confederate army, and where the younger
men have all their lives long drunk in endless tales
told by their elders, at home and at the cross-roads

taverns and in the court-house squares, about the cavalry of Forrest and Morgan and the infantry of Jackson and Hood. The blood of the older men stirred to the distant breath of battle; the blood of the younger men leaped hot with eager desire to accompany us. The older women, who remembered the dreadful misery of war—the misery that presses its iron weight most heavily on the wives and the little ones—looked sadly at us; but the young girls drove down in bevies, arrayed in their finery, to wave flags in farewell to the troopers and to beg cartridges and buttons as mementoes. Everywhere we saw the stars and stripes and everywhere we were told, half-laughing, by grizzled ex-Confederates, that they had never dreamed in the by-gone days of bitterness to greet the old flag as they now were greeting it, and to send their sons as they now were sending them to fight and die under it.

While the horses were being fed, Captain Heuston gave me permission to ride in the baggage car where I could make a good bed. On entering the car I found that we had been joined by four new men. Among them was "Bob" Wren, Harvard '95, formerly champion tennis player of America, and considered the best all around athlete in the United States. "Bob" is a ruddy-faced, cheerful fellow and ought to make a good man. With him were three friends, "Teddy" Burke of New York, "Bill" Larned, another crack tennis player, and Theodore Miller, Yale '97, who is a son of Lewis Miller, the founder of the Chautauqua work and a brother-in-law of Thomas Edison, the famous electrician.

After feeding the horses we left about 2:30 p. m. Harry Holt came out to the baggage car towards evening feeling quite sick so I helped the boys take care of him.

WEDNESDAY, JUNE 1ST.

We are quite short on rations now, as we only started with three days' rations and this is the fourth day. We fed the stock at Tallahassee, Florida, to-day. While in Mobile I saw the torpedo boat Du Pont which had run in for repairs, having been with the fleet off Santiago for nearly three weeks. The Fifth Cavalry, which is just ahead of us, had five horses ham-strung last night, probably the work of some Spanish sympathizer. In consequence we have a double guard on our horses, with instructions "to shoot to kill." This begins to sound something like war.

THURSDAY, JUNE 2ND.

We did not arrive in Tampa until midnight, and after unloading our horses we bivouaced beside the track until morning, many of the men sleeping under the cars to keep out of the dew. As we were short of men, I volunteered to go on guard and with loaded gun I walked my beat outside the sleeping camp until dawn.

FRIDAY, JUNE 3RD.

As day was beginning to break in the east reveille was sounded, and after a hasty breakfast of hardtack and water we mounted and rode into Tampa. The regiments with which we are to serve are already in camp, and the sandy streets of the little town are thronged with soldiers, almost all of them regulars, for there are but one or two volunteer organizations besides ourselves. The regulars wear the canonical, dark blue of Uncle Sam. However, as the Rough Riders trotted down the long, sandy street clad in their dusty brown blouses and trousers with leggins to match, and soft campaign hats, they looked very

workmanlike. We rode through the dusty town and
pitched our camp about a mile beyond the big Tampa
Bay Hotel on a sandy tract of pine land. Under
Colonel Wood's directions we put our tents up in
long streets, the picket line of each troop stretching
down its side of the street. The officers' quarters are
at the upper ends of the streets and the kitchens and
sinks at the opposite end. As Harry and I decided
to each take a Western man as bunkie during the
campaign, I am now bunking with "Lon" Muxlow
of Guthrie, Oklahoma. Lon is a fine fellow. He has
been a preacher, ranchman and prospector and in
every way is a typical Western man. As soon as we
got our tents up I got a pass and went over to Tampa
to get a bath and shave. I found the huge winter
hotel gay with general officers and their staffs, with
women in pretty dresses, with newspaper corres-
pondents by the score, and with military attaches of
foreign powers. After a bath and a large bowl of
bread and milk I returned to camp feeling much
better. Soon after my return I was accosted by a
young man in uniform who introduced himself as
Frank Knox of Grand Rapids. He said he had been
in Tampa two weeks with the Thirty-second Michigan
but would like to get into the Rough Riders. He said
he could ride and shoot and as I knew that we were
going to lose a few men on account of sickness I told
him I would speak to the Colonel. Hoping to find
Hoskins of Grand Rapids, whom I knew was with
the Thirty-second, I went out to their camp with
Knox and not only saw Hoskins, who appeared very
homesick, but also Warren Morrell of Benton Harbor.
After a refreshing swim in the bay I returned to
camp and saw Colonel Roosevelt in regard to Knox.
He said there were nine vacancies but he desired to
fill them with regulars if possible. However he

finally told me to bring Knox around in the morning and he would look him over.

Knox put in an early appearance this morning, and hunting up Roosevelt at headquarters, he was soon enrolled as a D trooper. Muxlow and I made room for him in our tent and he will stay with us until we land in Cuba, then I have promised to bunk with him although I hate to leave Muxlow.

We put in a good share of the day drilling on foot in order to rest our horses. The woods are filled with regiments at drill, there being about four thousand soldiers in camp. It is a fine sight to see two or three thousand cavalry advancing through the palmettoes, the red and white guidons fluttering at the fore, and the horses sweeping on in a succession of waves, as though they were being driven forward by the wind.

After reveille this morning we were ordered to clean up camp for inspection. This meant that our blankets must be folded in a certain way, saddle, bridle and picket rope in a certain position and everything as clean as possible. About eight o'clock General Wheeler, who is in command of the entire cavalry division of nine thousand men, rode through camp with Colonel Wood, making the inspection. General Wheeler is a very small man with a white beard, but he sits his horse very soldierly. It must seem strange to him to wear the blue after fighting so long for the grey. About ten we had church service conducted by Chaplain Brown who gave us a very good talk. After church Lieutenant Goodrich took a party of us over to the bay, some three miles

away, where we all had a fine swim.   We could see
the long line of transports at Port Tampa very plainly
and we all wished we were aboard.

CHAPTER II.

WEDNESDAY, JUNE 6TH.

At last the order to move has come. We have been notified that the expedition is to start for destination unknown at once and that we are one of the volunteer regiments chosen to go with the regulars. But our horses are to be left behind and only eight troops of seventy men each are to be taken. Our sorrow at leaving the horses is entirely outweighed by our joy at going. Major Brodie and Lieutenant Colonel Roosevelt are to command the two squadrons which are going. Luckily D troop is one of the troops to go and Captain Heuston has promised to take both Knox and myself. The horses and remaining men are to join us within two weeks, so we will probably have our horses before we do much fighting.

An infantryman came over this evening in order to show us how to roll our packs, for as we are to act as dismounted cavalry, each man has got to carry his belongings on his back. The roll is made by first putting half the shelter tent on the ground, then putting the blanket on the tent and putting other necessary articles on the blanket. The whole is then rolled up and the two ends brought together or nearly together forming a horse shoe shaped roll, which is then thrown over our left shoulder, coming across our breasts and under our right arms. Our mess kits and cup are carried by the hooks on our cartridge belts. We got our tents down and slept on our rolls ready to march.

TUESDAY JUNE 7TH.

Cleaned up camp this morning and divided the men into squads. Each squad consists of ten or a dozen men in charge of a sergeant and corporal. I am in sergeant Reay's squad with Hill as corporal. Unluckily Knox was put in Sergeant Hill's squad so we are separated for a time. In the evening we marched to Tampa and drew our pay at the hotel. I received $14.05. On our return to camp an artist for Scribners Magazine took our pictures in marching order. Knox is the eighth man from the end and I am the ninth. About ten o'clock we left camp and marched over to the railroad tracks but as no train came we slept on the road on our rolls all night.

WEDNESDAY, JUNE 8TH.

Knox and I made our first foraging expedition this morning. We awoke stiff and hungry and seeing a "canteen" started for it but there were so many ahead of us that it was in danger of being sold out before we could buy anything, so Knox helped me over the counter and I helped myself to cheese, crackers and lemonade. We then returned to the troop and divided up with some less fortunate ones. About six o'clock a train of dirty coal cars came along. This Roosevelt seized and in about half an hour we arrived at Port Tampa, covered with coal dust but with all our belongings. The dock was covered with soldiers, and in the long canal some thirty huge transports lay, loading men and supplies, while out in the bay a gun boat or two steamed lazily to and fro. After standing in the blazing sun for nearly an hour, we were double quicked down to where transport No 8, formerly the Yucutan, lay. We found four companies of the 2nd regular infantry already aboard, making nearly a

thousand men on a boat hardly capable of holding half
that number. D troop luckily was given a place on
the upper deck, starboard side, just forward of the
stern. We barely had room enough to lie down and
on account of the narrow space between the side of the
cabin and rail we could not stretch out full length.
However this was of small importance compared with
the fact that we were really embarked and were with
the first expedition to leave our shores. After loading
the transport which took all the rest of the day as
owing to the confusion our train had been unloaded at
the end of the dock furtherest from the ship, we pulled
off and anchored in midstream. Our travel rations we
find are not sufficient because the meat is very bad
indeed, and when a ration consists of only four or five
items, which taken together just meet the requirements
of a strong and healthy man, the loss of one item is a
serious thing. If we had been given canned corn beef
we would have been all right, but instead of this we
have been issued horrible stuff called "canned fresh
beef." There is no salt in it. At the best it is stringy
and tasteless; at the worst it is nauseating. Besides
this there is no ice, and the water we have for drinking is brackish and not even fit to wash in.

THURSDAY, JUNE 9TH.

Among the four companies of the 2nd regular
infantry on aboard, I found quite a number of Michigan boys, three of them being from Paw Paw   Harry
and I had a fine swim this morning going in off the
transport as we are permitted to morning and evening.
Tonight we are back in the harbor again and it is
reported that our sailing has been postponed on account
of some Spanish war vessels that have been sighted off
the Northern coast of Cuba. We were all interested
in watching a detail from one of the war vessels lay

a line of torpedoes or mines at the mouth of the canal this evening.

FRIDAY, JUNE 10TH.

We are still inside the canal with the gun boat "Castine" guarding the entrance. The canal presents quite a crowded scene as all the transports, some thirty in number are inside. It is rumored that all out-going mail is to be held five days in order to keep our movements a secret until we have landed on the coast of Cuba. There is a good deal of speculation in regards to our destination. Some think we are to be landed in Porto Rico while others think we are to take Santiago de Cuba. I myself believe that our destination is Santiago for when the city falls the fleet which is said to be in the harbor must either give our fleet a fight or be captured with the city.

SATURDAY, JUNE 11TH.

During the night five war ships ran into the bay and are now "lying to" near the outer entrance. We sailed out into the bay this morning and are apparently ready to sail. I hope we do so soon as this life, cooped up as we are without a chance to exercise, is becoming monotonous.

We received the first mail since the 6th today and accordingly are in good spirits. I received ten letters and a whole bundle of papers. Towards evening the war vessels coaled up and put to sea, and as the sailors on board the transports have been busy all the afternoon tightening the rigging it looks as if we might sail tonight.

SUNDAY, JUNE 12TH.

This morning the fleet of war vessels returned and are now peacefully lying at anchor in the bay. Services were held on the after-deck this morning by the Chaplain of the Second Infantry. In the afternoon Colonel Roosevelt gave us one of his characteristic talks which we all enjoyed. We received some back mail to day which had been forwarded from San Antonio.

MONDAY, JUNE 13TH.

An order to move was received this morning. When Colonel Roosevelt heard the news he could not restrain himself and entertained us all by giving an impromptu war dance. Last night we had a terrific rain storm which flooded the decks and soaked us all. As there was an inspection at noon we were kept busy cleaning our guns all the morning for the rain had rusted them badly. At four o'clock we weighed anchor and went slowly ahead under half steam for the distant mouth of the harbor, the bands playing, the flags flying, the rigging black with clustered soldiers, cheering and shouting to those left behind and to the fellows on the other ships. The channel was very tortuous, and we anchored before we had gone far down it, after coming within an ace of a bad collision with another transport.

TUESDAY, JUNE 14TH.

At daylight we were under way again and soon passed the bar and were at last out on the broad Atlantic, and as Tampa light sank in the distance we bad farewell to the United States—some of us perhaps forever.

The thirty odd transports are moving in long parallel lines, while ahead and behind and on their flanks the gray hulls of the warships are surging through the wonderful sapphire seas of the West Indies. We have every variety of craft to guard us, from the mighty battleship and the swift cruisers to the converted yachts and the frail venomous looking torpedo boats.

The City of Washington, which was so near the Maine at the time of her destruction, sails next to us in the fleet of transports. Disease is already making its appearance on board the crowded transports. We now have three cases of measles on board the Yucatan but nothing can prevent the men being in good spirits for at last we are on our way to Cuba. We do not know exactly where we are bound, nor what we are to do. But we are confident that the nearing future holds for us many chances of death, of hardship, of honor and renown. If we fail we shall meet the fate of all who fail. But we believe we will win and that we shall score the first great triumph in a mighty world-movement. At night we lie on the decks and look at new stars and hail the Southern Cross. In the daytime we drill or scan the wonderful blue sea and watch the flying fish. In the evening the Second Infantry band plays tune after tune on our forward deck, until on our quarter the glorious sun sinks in the red west, and, one by one the lights blaze out on our troop-ship and warship for miles ahead and astern, as they steam onward through the tropic night.

WEDNESDAY, JUNE 15TH.

After a wild and windy night we awoke this morning to find ourselves far out at sea with no land in sight. During the night a new battleship joined us; she is said to be the Oregon commanded by Captain Clark and just arrived from her wonderful trip around the Horn. Our present course is southwest. It is very pleasant sailing through the tropic seas towards the unknown. The men of the ship are young and strong, and we are eager to face what lies before us, eager for adventure where risk is the price of gain.

It is interesting to listen to the Western fellows, loung-
ing in groups, and telling stories of their past—stories
of the mining camps and the cattle ranges, of hunting
bear and deer, of war trails against the Indians, of lawless deeds of violence and the lawful violence by which
they were avenged, of brawls in saloons, of shrewd
deals in cattle and sheep, of successful quests for gold
and silver, stories of brutal wrong and brutal appetite,
melancholy love-tales and memories of nameless heroes
—masters of men and tamers of horses.

THURSDAY, JUNE 16TH.

At two o'clock last night we passed the Dry
Tortugas and sent mail ashore. During the night
Sampson's fleet of twelve war vessels joined us; there
are also several torpedo boats with us which are towed
behind armed tugs in order to save their fuel. At
dawn this morning our course was southeast. We
caught the first sight of the Cuban coast this afternoon,
a white light house on the outlying key of Paredon
Grande. At five o'clock I was placed on guard at
post number one in front of the Officers' quarters.
My instructions were to shoot at any boat approaching
nearer than thirty yards which did not answer my
challenge.

FRIDAY, JUNE 17TH.

Our course this morning is nearly east and I think
that we are in the Nicholas Channel, off the Northern
coast of Cuba. The mainland is now in view—hazy
hills rising above the blue sea. About noon we passed
a small open sail boat flying the Cuban flag and containing three men who wasted a good deal of amuni-
tion in saluting us. It was a mail boat carrying the
mail to Nassau. We now have daily drills on deck

by squads in command of the sergeants in aiming and volley firing.

SATURDAY, JUNE 18TH.

We had a very fine exhibition of fire works last night. The warships were signalling one another by means of colored rockets. This morning Frank Knox was added to my squad and he and I are now "bunkies."

SUNDAY, JUNE 19TH.

Our course this morning is east by south so we must be near the eastern end of Cuba. Services were held by our Chaplain on the after-deck this morning and Roosevelt also made a few remarks. At four o'clock our course was changed to south by east and we are now well in the Windward Passage. It is evident now that our destination is Santiago.

MONDAY, JUNE 20TH.

Cape Maysi was rounded last night and this morning the great, broken Sierras that lie along the southern coast of Cuba are in view. High mountains rise almost from the waters edge, looking huge and barren across the sea. But after so long a time aboard a transport, the shore, barren as it is, looks tempting. I cannot help but wonder what it has in store for me but am eager to land and get into a fight in order to find out what kind of stuff is in me. As I lay sunning myself on the hurricane deck this afternoon, the thought came to me that if I had not enlisted I would have taken my last examination today and tomorrow would probably have started for home. But I feel that I am where I ought to be and although the life is a hard one I would not return to college if I could for I could not then be true to my ideal.

At last we are in sight of the goal. Morro Castle and the entrance to Santiago harbor and the warships standing off it, gray and sullen in their war paint can be plainly seen off our bow. All day we have lain at anchor but we have been ordered to be ready to land in the morning. We are to land at Darquiri. Darquiri I understand is owned by an American mining company controlled by the Carnegie Corporation at Pittsburg. There seems to be a railroad wharf and a few huts at the landing place which is in a small cove. Behind these rise the mountains, and on a steep and lofty spur is a little Spanish block-house with a flag pole at its side.

The morning is cool and clear and there seems to be no sign of life in the village but the pier is on fire so it is evident the place is not deserted. About nine o'clock the bombardment began and in an instant the Oregon, Detroit, Castine, New Orleans and the little Wasp, which was directly in front of us and only a short mile away, were enveloped in smoke. The valleys sent back the reports of the guns in long, thundering echoes that reverberated again and again, and the mountain-side began at once to spurt up geysers of earth and branches of broken bushes. The block-house was demolished and the thatched shocks were soon bright bon fires. It was the grandest sight I ever witnessed and I could hardly realize that the shots were fired in anger and that the warships were searching for hidden batteries. Under cover of this heavy bombardment, we landed with no little risk on account of the high surf which threatened to dash our boats on the rocks. We stepped on dry ground with a great feeling of relief and stretched ourselves in a beautiful valley surrounded by huge mountains. We can hardly realize that this delightful place is the dreaded, tropical region of which we have heard so much. On the closer hills can be seen the long, shaggy leaves of the palm, the towering cocoanut trees lifting their fronded heads above the lower woods and in the distance a purple peak looms up. We were greeted on landing by a number of Castello's men who trooped down to the landing place with wild "vivias" to welcome the landing of the first of the armies of liberation. They were a motley looking crowd, big, black fellows with shiny bodies, most of them only half clad and some nearly naked, but they gave us a friendly greeting and disposed of all the hardtack we gave them in a manner most mysterious. We were marched but a few hundred yards from shore, when after a supper of hardtack and beans we were ordered to sleep on our rolls with our guns within easy reach. It was cold and damp but at last I dropped off to sleep, the ground making a soft bed after the deck of the transport.

THURSDAY, JUNE 23RD.

This morning men are still landing and everywhere squads of regulars can be seen hurrying to and fro. About seven thousand landed last night so there are about nine thousand yet to land. The Cuban troops are marching to the front and create considersble amusement by their dress. One old fellow as black as the "ace of spades" marched by this morning with only an artillery overcoat on, one he had stolen from our camp. The sweat was rolling down his naked body and yet he kept the heavy overcoat on with the bright red cape thrown back over his shoulder. The Cuban women present quite a contrast to the ones we are accustomed to see in the United States. The first native hut I visited last night contained three olive skinned girls who had nothing on but short skirts. Thinking I had intruded as they were about to retire I beat a hasty retreat, but this morning I find that very few of the women are more than half dressed, a cotton skirt reaching to the knees constituting the only garment of the majority and the children play around in the dirt entirely naked but seemingly happy.

Burgess and I went down to the creek this morning and after filtering some water through the sand to get rid of yellow fever germs, as there is said to be a fever hospital directly above us, had a very refreshing bath. Soap is a very scarce article, but luckily I have some in my toilet case.

It is very warm and the men who are not foraging after cocoanuts which are very plentiful, are busy making shelters of palm leaves, for we have not yet received orders to put our tents up. Some of the palm leaves are ten feet long.

CHAPTER III.

The Fight at Guasimas.

About three o'clock "general call sounded" and
soon we were on the march and marched along a
narrow trail scarcely wide enough for two men. The
pace was so brisk, that after the first three miles the
intense heat began to tell and man after man dropped
out, over-come by the heat. Our march was like a
pipe organ having many stops. We were in full
marching order, that means each man carries a carbine, a hundred rounds of ammunition, canteen,
poncho, half a shelter tent, an army blanket, rations
and other necessary articles that we were obliged to
have. As we struggled up the hillsides and tramped
down the slopes, the packs shifted and slipped and
bore down on our aching shoulders. As the sun beat
down on us the packs and bundles slid about as
though they were alive and gained in weight from
pounds to tons. In the woods the packs caught in
overhanging underbrush and sent us stumbling and
falling. In the open places the sun was like a fur-
nace and the packs were like lead. At last we could
stand it no longer and we began to throw away our
blankets; after the blankets went cans of meat, then
our coats and underclothes until some only had their
guns and ammunition left, for these were essentials.
At last we marched into Siboney and encamped beyond the fartherest outposts of the infantry. It was

then we realized we had been racing; racing to get to the front ahead of Lawton and his infantry for General Wheeler had determined that the cavalry should be the first to fight. When the infantry marched into Siboney, the Spaniards fled setting fire to many of the buildings and the railroad bridge. We had marched a good ten miles and only about half the men went into camp with us; the rest were left along the trail, some in convulsions and some unconscious from the heat. Knox and I pulled through on our nerve alone. As soon as we struck camp, we stripped and gave each other a thorough massage, then we went down to the bay only a few feet away and had a fine swim in the cool ocean. Men were now landing at Siboney and the war ships with their search lights turned on made Siboney as light as a ball room. Back of the search lights was an ocean white with moonlight and on shore red camp fires at which the half drowned men were drying their uniforms and the Rough Riders cooking their coffee. Cunningham of my troop had a fit just as we made camp and Teddy Miller seems to have entirely lost his reason, the exertion of the march being too much for them.

The scene is a most weird and remarkable one. An army is being landed on an enemy's coast in the dead of night. On either side rise black overhanging ridges; in the lowlands between are white tents and burning fires, and from the ocean comes the blazing, dazzling eyes of the searchlights shaming the quiet moonlight.

FRIDAY, JUNE 24TH.

After a troubled sleep in wet clothes, for it rained hard just as we made camp, we were aroused about 2:30 by reveille. It was as dark as pitch and it seemed as if I had hardly closed my eyes. Our shoulders were sore from the heavy packs, and our legs stiff from the march of the day before. Men who had kept their packs the day before began to realize that lots of useful articles were not needed and in consequence everything but the barest necessities were thrown away, even the blankets were split in half, for two nights ashore had convinced us that if the days were hot the nights were cold. All during the day not even the livliest imagination could conceive of such heat could be followed by any such poetic relief as the "cool of the evening" nor were the evenings cool, but it was at that crisis of the night, the early hours of dawn, that the searching, penetrating cold came upon us. So cold indeed was it at this time, partly by comparison with the hot day and partly as a positive condition, that we were actually awakened, shivering about two or three o'clock.

After a hasty breakfast we fell in for roll call, and with ranks sadly depleted by yesterday's march, we started up over a long steep hill. The sun was hot and soon men began to fall out, but Knox and I having lightened our packs kept in the column for Knox had heard Colonel Wood say that we would smell powder today and we both wanted to be in at least the first fight. The only thing that worried us was the fear that the Spaniards would retreat without fighting.

We find the flying pests of Cuba bad enough but I believe it is the consensus of opinion that bad as gnats, mosquitoes and beetles are, we dread them less than the land craps and this because of the repulsiveness of the latter creatures. These hard shelled, crawling things are everywhere, in the woods and on the plains, crowds of them in the gullies and troops of them on the hill tops. No matter where we march or where we halt we find them. In size the land craps vary from four to twelve inches across the carapace, its covering area being increased by leg and claws, the latter quite formidable impliments. They are rather gay colored creatures, their tints ranging from light green to dark blue. They have the strange fashion of moving forward a few feet and then scuttling sideways. As they move they clash their claws and rattle among themselves.

After about three hours march, during which we passed by many deserted block houses, we were halted in a place where the trail was sunken. We sat down on the banks and talked and the men who smoked rolled cigarettes. We were discussing trivial affairs and joking or gazing wonderingly into the dense underbrush which surrounded us on all sides so thickly that it had been impossible to throw out flankers.

Troop L under Captain Capron was acting as advance for the regiment. Sergeant Hamilton Fish and four other men formed the point or scouting party and in advance of these was Isable of L troop with two Cuban scouts. Presently word was passed back to cease talking for the scouts had encountered the Spanish outposts. We were ordered to load chambers and magazines. It was hard for me to realize the actuality of the enemy and that I was on the verge of my first fight. The firing when it came started suddenly on our right and seemed so close that I thought it was Capron's men firing at random to locate the enemy. But as my troop was deployed through a gap in the fence on our left, I heard the bullets go zipping by my head and realized that the fight was on. The corner was an exceedingly hot one and the Spanish aim was so low that we were compelled to lie down and fire in that position. I found myself at the extreme flank of my troop with Burgess and Cashion on my right. As my troop was on the left flank I was on the extreme left flank of the battle formation. Lieutenant Goodrich walked up and down and behaved like a veteran. After the first shot my nervousness disappeared and I was as calm as if shooting quail. The only thing that troubled me was that only now and then could I see a Spaniard and those I did see were on a distant ridge. We advanced through a net work of tangled grape vines and bushes. our packs were strewn on the hill side, the water in our canteens was gone and enemy's fire got hotter and hotter. Captain Capron, Fish, Russell and Doherty fell. Newcomb, Ishler, Beal and Rhodes of D troop were carried to the rear wounded But all the men seemed cool and determined no one paid any attention when the man next to him was badly wounded or perhaps killed. That seemed to come as a matter of course which did not excite more interest than a finger out of joint in a football game.

Burgess and I found we were under a heavy cross fire and concluded that F troop must be firing on us from the rear. We called to them but the fire only grew hotter. We lost our own troop in the tangled brush. Burgess left me to tend to a wounded man as he was a "First Aid" man. I joined G troops under Greenway and saw two men fall mortally wounded. At last we charged and as the firing grew more and more distant we realized that the day was won without our having hardly seen the enemy. I started to look up my troop when I came across poor Doherty of B troop shot through the head; his chest was heaving with a short, hoarse noise which I guessed was due to some muscular action, and that he was virtually dead. I called a surgeon and we started to the rear with him when suddenly I felt dizzy and would have fallen if the surgeon had not caught me. Quickly opening his case he poured some "spirits of ammonia" down my throat and I felt better at once. He ordered me to the hospital saying that I had narrowly missed a sun stroke.

I started down the narrow, blood besprinkled trail and passed the bodies of Capron and Fish lying cold in death. I soon found D troop and reported to Captain Heuston and was immediately placed on a skirmish line. I fond Knox and Harry Holt all right and learned that we had lost four men, all wounded, in D troop. I now began to feel faint and Lieutenant Carr told me to go up to a temporary hospital which was located in a stone distillery which had just been deserted by the Spaniards. Cashion asked me for my cup in order to get some water in it for me and I found a bullet hole had rendered it useless. It hung on my belt during battle and in the excitement I did not notice that it had been struck. As I lie in the hospital I can see Lawton's infantry marching to the front; they all feel chagrined to think we beat them and got into the first fight. I learn we have lost fifty-three wounded and eight killed, and the 1st and 10th regular cavalry who were engaged with us on the other side of the trail lost eight killed and twenty wounded. About sunset the regiment marched into camp leaving me alone in the deserted hospital. Knox and Cunningham shared their blankets with me as I had lost everything in the fight. The 2nd Massachusetts infantry is camped next to us and they seem to think we play our part well. After a cold supper I turned in.

SATURDAY, JUNE 25TH.

This morning I was detailed to go over the battle field and looked for the wounded and killed that have not been brought in, as several are missing; however we only found a sew packs. It was a sight to see the trees on the battle field all cut to pieces by bullets. We saw several dead Spaniards that had not been buried. However the vultures will make short work of them. We returned to camp just in time to witness the funeral services over our dead. It was the most impressive services I ever saw. The bodies were all placed in one long trench and covered with huge palm leaves before any dirt was thrown in. As the grave was being filled in the regiment joined in singing "Nearer My God to Thee." This is our first funeral and tears came to the eyes of the most hardened as the trumpet sounded "Taps" over the last long sleep of our brave comrades. The men may have laughed and joked in battle but here they stood silent and choking.

The remainder of the day we spent resting. I had some of my letters from my pack returned to me this afternoon by a regular army officer. I shall keep them as mementos. He found them on a field where my pack had been cut open by Cubans. The Cubans not only let us do all the fighting but robed us of all our rations so we had to wait until nearly midnight for something to eat as our pack train did not come up until then.

INCIDENTS.

It is reported that the Spaniards numbered between two and three thousand men while our force, counting the troops of the First and Tenth Cavalry only numbered nine hundred and ten men, our entire loss being sixteen killed and seventy-three wounded, the Rough Riders suffering over half of the entire loss.

It is said that the Cubans have tried again and again to take this pass but have been unable to do so, while we captured the Spanish position in two hours and a half.

Officers like General Wheeler, who have seen

service before, say that the firing was very hot and that it was remarkable to see men advance right in the face of such a heavy fire.

Sal Newcomb, Fred Beal, Corporal Rhodes and Ishler are the names of those wounded in my troop. Little Corporal Denham is probably mortally shot, the bullet passing through the base of the spine.

The regulars as they pass our camp going towards the front, cheer us with congratulations on the showing we have made in the first fight, but we continually think of the dead and count our victory dearly won.

CHAPTER IV.

The Advance on Santiago.

SUNDAY, JUNE 26TH.

This being Sunday of course we had to move. It seems as if Sunday is the favorite day for breaking camp. At eight this morning we broke camp and marched two miles under a blazing sun to a new camping place with sweeter odors, for we have learned from experience that a battle field is not the best camping ground imaginable. We are now camped in a marshy, open spot, close to a beautiful stream of water. From the hills at the foot of which we are camped the city of Santiago, with its red tile roofs glistening in the sun, can be plainly seen. We are under very strict orders about leaving camp, always have to have our canteens full and our guns handy. We cannot even go after water without permission. Whenever we "fall in" we must have our cartridge belts and canteens on, and at night we must have our guns by our sides.

We were visited by some "tars" from Sampson's fleet today; they had come ten miles to see the Rough Riders of whom they had heard so much. I guess they found us a rather disappointing sight for while they were immaculate in their white uniforms, we were clad in only rough blue shirts, ragged trousers and muddy leggins. Our campaign hats were torn and out of shape, while none of us had bathed for a

week, for now we have to sleep with even our cartridge belts on and we can only use water from our
canteens to wash from while few of us have any soap.
The tars said when we got ready they would bombard he city and all we would have to do would be
to capture the "dons" as they came out.

· The rainy season has apparently set in for every
afternoon now the rain comes down in such torrents
that our shelter tents are but scant protection. I
never saw it rain like it does here; after every rain
the trails are turned into torrents and our camp ground
into a quagmire.

A Spanish spy was captured this morning and
after his trial he was turned over to the Cubans who
beheaded him with their machetes. Knox and I are
trying hard to learn Spanish and can talk some with
the Cubans who hang around camp begging for what
they dare not steal.

MONDAY, JUNE 27TH.

General Shafter received a cablegram from
President McKinley today congratulating us on our
first fight. We are just beginning to learn that we
have made a reputation for ourselves. The Spaniards themselves did not question but what they
could defeat us at the "Pass" where they had so
many times defeated the Cubans, but our steady
advance nonplussed them.

It has been two weeks now since we have
received any mail and we are all anxious to move on
the city so the mail boat will have a harbor. The
army is camped along the valley, ahead of and
behind us, our outposts being established on either
side. We are all eager to march on Santiago. At
day break when the tall palms begin to show dimly
through the rising mist, the tropic dawn is torn by

the cavalry trumpets, and we fall in for roll call; and in the evening as the band of regiment after regiment plays the "Star Spangled Banner, all the officers and men alike stand with heads uncovered wherever they are until the last strains of the anthem dies away in the hot sunset air.

We are not given quite the proper amount of food, and what we do get is like the clothing issued, fitter for the Klondike than for Cuba. We get enough hardtack and salt pork but not the full ration of coffee and sugar and nothing else. I got some Mangoes today and cooked them into jelly and they were very good. The Mango is a tropical food something like a plum and is said to cause a good deal of sickness, but we are willing to take the risk after living so long on hardtack and salt pork.

TUESDAY, JUNE 28TH.

Four batteries of light artillery under Captian Capron are camped opposite us now and other batteries are coming up. I was put on the road building detail today and worked with pick and shovel for six hours. There is about six inches of sticky mud in the road and it is almost impossible to get the guns up. General Shafter and staff rode up today. Shaf- ter looked like he could carry the mule he was riding on better than the mule could carry him. He is an enormous man weighing about 320 pounds.

It is so hot that cooking is exceedingly disagree- able, besides wood fit for a camp fire is very scarce. Knox and I generally cook enough in the early morning to last all day. I made a hard tack pudding today which did not prove to be a great success.

WEDNESDAY, JUNE 29TH.

At inspection this morning we received orders to eat no native fruits raw or cooked as they are conducive to the fever. Last night the cruisers Harvard and Yale landed at Siboney with reinforcements. Among the new troops are the 33rd and 34th Michigan, so I hope to see some of the boys from home soon.

It is reported that our horses will soon come over and that after Santiago falls the cavalry under General Wheeler will march across Cuba and join Lee in time to participate in the fighting around Havana, while the infantry will go to Porto Rico.

As day succeeds day, we grow more and more anxious for our mail as we have received none since landing in Cuba.

THURSDAY, JUNE 30TH.

A war balloon came up this morning. It is to be used in reconnoitering the defenses of the city. Everything is moving towards the front. Mule train after mule train is being pushed forward with supplies and ammunition, and it looks as if a heavy battle is expected. The men are all eager for the struggle and will not need much urging. The rations are still short and are beginning to get tiresome. Coffee and hardtack three times a day is not much to look forward to. Having run out of wood, Knox and I got permission and went up on the hillside this morning and cut wood enough for a week.

3 P. M.

We have just received marching orders and have only thirty minutes to break camp in. Four days rations have been issued.

9 P. M.

After breaking camp, we marched about six miles through a thick jungle and under a hot sun and are now camped on El Paso hill near the ruins of an

old ranch and within three miles of Santiago, which
we can plainly see.   While we were on the march
we saw the war balloon go up ahead of us.   It is
evident that we are near the enemy, for no fires are
allowed and no bugle calls are given.   We are
ordered to sleep on the ground without our tents, and
to maintain our troop formation.   We have a very
heavy picket out tonight and no noises are permitted.
It is evident that there will be lots of fun for us in the
morning.

CHAPTER V.

The San Juan Fight, July 1st, 2nd and 3rd.

FRIDAY, JULY 1ST.

The stars were still shining this morning when Captain Heuston shook my shoulder and told me to hurry up and get something to eat. While we were eating a large force of Cubans in all stages of undress filed by on their way to the front. As the sun rose we "fell in" and at the same time a battery of field guns came up. A short consultation was held, and then it was determined to plant the guns on the crest of the hill and open fire. It was a fine sight to see the great horses straining under the lash as they whirled the guns up the hill and into position, the men using whip, spur and oaths freely and all at once, and the officers riding alongside waving their arms wildly, shouting words of instruction and encouragement.

It was about six o'clock when the report of a cannon came booming across the miles of still jungle on our left. It was Capron opening the fight at El Caney on our left flank. It was a very lovely morning, the sky cloudless blue while the level shimmering rays from the just-risen sun brought into fine relief the splendid palms which here and there towered above the lower growth. The lofty and beautiful mountains hemmed in the Santiago plain making as it were an amphitheatre for the battle.

Immediately our guns opened, and at the report
great clouds of white smoke hung on the ridge crest.
Several guns were fired with no response from the
Spaniards. Suddenly there was a peculiar whistling
sound in the air and immediately afterwards the
noise of something exploding over our heads, It was
a shrapnel from the Spanish batteries. Immediately
afterwards a second shot came and burst directly
above us, and then a third which exploded right
among a lot of Cubans, killing and wounding a great
many any wounding some of the Rough Riders.
Shell after shell came shrieking toward us. Some of
the gunners were killed and we were hustled over
the crest of the hill and ordered to lie down. As the
Spanish batteries used smokeless powder their
artillery had an immense advantage over ours, and
moreover, our guns were not of the best type and
our fire very slow. Meanwhile on our left we could
hear the roll of musketry at El Caney and knew that
the battle there was hot. Soon we received marching orders, and in column of fours marched down the
road toward the ford of the San Juan river, passing
several regiments on our way. The trail was lined
with dead horses torn by shells, and I saw several
punctured canteens. The Spaniards in the trenches
on the hill were already firing at us in desultory
fashion. The war balloon was now sent up directly
over us. This offered an especial target to the
enemy; when it reached the fort it collapsed, and,
hanging from a tree caused considerable loss of life
for it indicated the ford where the Ninth and Tenth
Cavalry were crossing. We huddled together under
the bank of the San Juan River, for some time standing in water up to our middle, but thankful to be
out of range of the bullets and shells which continually tore through the trees. Soon wounded men

were brought down under the shelter of the bank. Captain Bucky O'Niel was killed about twenty yards ahead of me and the fight was now on in good earnest. The Spaniards on the hills were engaged in volley firing. The mauser bullets drove in sheets through the trees and tall jungle grass making a peculiar whining or rustling sound. Some of the bullets seemed to pop in the air so that we thought they were explosive. The Spanish fire seemed to sweep the whole field of battle up to the edge of the river and man after man in our ranks fell dead or wounded although we were taking advantage of every scrap of cover. At last we were deployed on a skirmish line and advanced through the heavy jungle, sometimes running and sometimes crawling. We passed several regiments of regulars lying down. The guerrillas were shooting at us from the edges of the jungle and from their perches in the leafy trees. As it was almost impossible to see them, we were unable to respond.

We soon ran into the left wing of the Ninth Regulars and some of the First Regulars lying down. Roosevelt, after consulting with their officers led us through their ranks and ordered us to charge the hill in front, Kettle Hill.

This proved too much for the Regulars for they jumped up and followed us up the hill. We crossed a small stream and started up the slope, but the Spaniards now retreated to the next line of hills which is called the San Juan range. We stopped about a hundred yards from the crest to re-form our line and get breath, for the sun was hot and the men were already becoming exhausted. We lay here about half an hour exchanging shots with the Spaniards who were strongly entrenched on the hill in front of us. Along the hill were several strong, stone block houses and these were our objective. All of the Spaniards were in their entrenchments showing only their heads as they raised to fire, but several officers walked up and down encouraging their men. One mounted on a black horse furnished an excellent mark until he was wounded. This lying still in plain sight of the enemy was to me the most trying part of the battle. To lie quietly with bullets pecking up the dust two or three feet away from one is at least hard on the nerves. It was therefore with a feeling of relief that we made the final charge, which we did at the double quick, the Spaniards doing some heavy volley firing until we started up the hill and then retreating hurriedly to the city. We lost a good many men in this charge but we found the Spanish trenches filled with dead and one live trumpeter playing possom. Some one discovered him and pulled him out. He was so terrified he could scarcely stand up. He fully expected to be shot or stabbed immediately. Lieutenant Greenway took his bugle and then sent him to the rear under-guard. Several other Spaniards were captured in this way, and we immediately put them to work carrying our wounded to the field hospital.

After a good rest Colonel Roosevelt led us across the plateau at "the double" up to the very crest of the hill that overlooked the city. This last charge was the prettiest of all for the country being open the men kept a good line, kneeling now and then to fire. From the crest of the hill we could look right down on to the Spanish entrenchments barely three hundred yards away. We were unable to advance further on account of the heavy underbrush which was at the foot of the hill and in front of the Spanish entrenchments. As we were exposed to a very fierce fire here our loss was heavy. Cashion, the youngest boy in the regiment, was shot between the eyes as he lay not two feet from me, and Corporal Meagher on the other side was wounded in the shoulder. Orders then came to withdraw a few yards and hold the hills with intrenchments. As we fell back some of the negroes in the Ninth and Tenth Cavalry became demoralized and Colonel Roosevelt said he would shoot any man who left the hill without permission. He said his orders were to hold the hill and he would obey them until the last man fell. After we fell back about fifty yards just over the crest of the hill we were safe if we lay flat on the ground and did not raise our heads for the bullets coming over the crest passed about three or four inches above us, cutting the grass on all sides. In order not to draw the Spanish fire and to save our ammunition which was very short we were ordered to cease firing.

After lying some time I thought I would take a look over the crest; on raising my head I saw a group of three Spanish Officers on horseback riding along the Spanish lines. Obtaining permission from Lieutenant Carr I crawled out in front of our lines and opened up on them; at the third shot with my sights raised to five hundred yards the officer in the center fell from his horse. As I was the only one shooting at him it must have been my bullet that killed him.

About five o'clock above the cracking of the carbines rose a peculiar, drumming sound and some of the men cried "The Spanish machine guns." But Roosevelt jumping to his feet cried, "It's the gatlings men, our gatlings." Lieutenant Parker was bringing his four gatlings into action and shoving them nearer and nearer the front. Now and then the drumming ceased for a moment; then it would resound again always closer to the front I can frankly say that I never heard a more welcome sound than those gatlings as they opened. We could not refrain from cheering the guns as they finally came into position on our line. The artillery had been silenced every time it opened but the gatlings using smokeless powder were not so easily located.

Finally darkness fell and never was night more welcome. Our thin line, having but one quarter its original strength, was completely tired out, for from early dawn until the sun set we had been fighting our way, inch by inch, over the roughest kind of country in a sun that seemed to blister our skin. We had none of us tasted a bit of food since early morning, and few of us had any water in our canteens. Our ammunition was gone and we were miles from the base of supplies with an entrenched enemy in front of us.

But if we expected to hold the hill there was but one thing to do and that was to entrench ourselves during the night. Luckily there was plenty of entrenching tools in the block houses we had captured. With these the men were set to work. Corporal Moran was detailed to put out a cassock post and he picked Cook, Byrnes and myself as pickets. As we went silently back to the block house on San Juan hill, we passed four or five dead Spaniards and quite a number of Rough Riders, their upturned faces looking ghastly in the bright moonlight. Securing picks and shovels we stole quietly out in front of our lines and while Cook and Moran kept watch Byrnes and I dug a pit large enough for three men right on the crest of the hill. We could hear the hurrying and scurring through the streets of the city and wondered if the Spaniards were deserting Santiago. After digging the first pit we dug a second large enough for one person about fifteen yards in front of the first. Moran then put Cook out in this pit and the three of us lay shivering in the second pit. In an hour Cook was relieved by Byrnes and then at twelve o'clock I took my turn. It was a terrible strain to have the safety of so many men depending on you alone. and I could not help but think of home and wonder what would happen to me if the Spaniards charged us for between their fire and the fire from our own lines we would have little chance of escape with our lives. As I peered into the brush on all sides of me, the lines of the poem, "All is quiet along the Potomac tonight. Only a stray picket shot now and then," kept running through my head. I was glad when Cook relieved me at the end of the hour but at three I had to go out again and Moran told me that if the Spaniards made a charge they would make it before long for the night is always darkest just before the break of day. He warned me to be on the alert and not go to sleep. I went out munching a hardtack and piece of raw bacon that Lieutenant Goodrich had given me while inspecting the outposts; this was the first food I had had since early the previous morning and I was ravenously hungry. I had not been on post long when I thought I heard the brush crackle in front of me. Cocking my carbine I glanced along the barrel and found to my dismay that the night was so dark that it was impossible to see the sights. Every little while I could hear a twig break and felt confident a scout was near, so when Cook relieved me I informed him of my suspicions and had barely got back into the pit when crack went Cook's carbine, and a dog yelped two or three times as if hurt. We heard a loud crackling in the bush, then all was still.

Suddenly all along the line firing began and continued for some time. When Cook was relieved he said he had seen two heads but fired low and evidently hit a dog that was with the scouts.

Soon grey streaks began to appear in the east and we knew that the terrible strain was over and that the welcome day was at hand. Sharpshooters soon began to open up on us and things were getting unconfortable. As we could not withdraw without orders, Moran crawled back and got permission to bring us in. By this time it was quite light and I for one would about as soon have stayed in the pit as to try and cross the open space necessary in order to regain our lines. But we had to get back, so we all started on the dead run, running zigzag and with our bodies bent almost double. The minute we started the Spaniards opened up on us as we were in plain view from their entrenchments, and the bullets hummed around our ears fiercely for a few minutes. But we reached our lines and threw ourselves down in safety.

SATURDAY, JULY 2ND.

The battle was now on again and with a vengeance too. A perfect hail of bullets came over the hill and the batteries in the city, and the ships in the harbor opened on us with shrapnel. Poor Stanley Hollister was struck by a piece of shrapnel and had his sides torn open, the same shell killing or wounding half a dozen others. Stanley is the first of the Harvard men to get hit. The fire finally swept the hill so that all the men excepting those in the entrenchments were ordered half way down the slope. Here I found Lieutenant Carr lying on his back, half naked, with his parched tongue protruding from his mouth. Giving him some water from my canteen, as his contained nothing but some Spanish rum of which he already had too much, I finally got him to a realization of his condition. Just then Captain Mueller came up and ordered Byrnes, who was near, and myself to take the Lieutenant back to the rear.

Carrying him down the hill we found a Spanish Artillery mule which we had captured in the charge. Thinking to get Carr on the mule, we approached it but he said he would be unable to stay in the saddle so with Byrnes supporting him on one side and I on the other, we started for the hospital which we knew was somewhere in the rear.

We soon got out from under cover of the hill and bullets begau to fly unpleasautly near, while now and then a shell would come shriekiug and hissing through the air. After going a short distance we were joined by a man who had been struck by a shell in the head. He presented a sickening sight with the blood stream·iug down his face, but we were used to such sights by this time. Hastily examing his wouuds, I put a bandage on and gave him a drink from my canteen. Then we started for the hospital again, but the wounded man was weak from the loss of blood and soon fell behind.

We had just climbed a barb wire fence and started across the field where we had formed our first skirmish line, when suddenly the Lieutenant who had one arm around my neck and one around Byrnes, exclaimed "My God! I am shot," and dropped to the ground. I had heard a chug as if a bullet had struck the ground uear and thought that the Lieutenant only imagined he was shot, but on making an examination we found that he really had been shot aud the wound was a very bad one in the groin. We were both surprised to fiud that the bullet had eutered from our front or in other words had been fired from the rear of the battle line, for at first we supposed it to be a spent bullet from the front. Naturally we supposed some of our own men had fired and that we had been mistaken for Spaniards, so Byrnes and I stood up and shouted out that we were Americans but

Obtained no answer. It was plain that the Lieutenant had to be carried now, so helping him to the road we dressed his wounds as well as we could and Byrnes started for help. A Surgeon soon came along and I asked him to dress the Lieutenant's wound properly. The Surgeon said that the Lieutenant had undoubtedly been shot by a Spanish sharpshooter as there were a number of them posted in trees back of our lines. So I started out to take a look around when whiz a bullet went by my head close enough to fully convince me the Surgeon was right. Thinking to fool the sharpshooter, I stood up and again he fired coming still closer; dropping as if killed I looked around and soon located the sharpshooter in a tree about three hundred yards away. Just then Byrnes came back with Harry Holt and Babcock of K troop. Showing them the sharpshooter I opened up. He seemed to drop on the limb at my first shot but returned my fire while Harry and Byrnes were trying to find their rifles. I fired three more times, taking careful aim each time, and finally he rolled off the limb. My firing had started several fusilades around us, and at the Lieutanant's request we remained where we were until things quited down. I found that Harry and Babcock were on wounded detail and had just carried poor Miller of D troop who was shot as we started up San Juan hill to the hospital. As they had half a shelter tent with them, we put the Lieutenant in that and wrapping our guns in two sides of it we improvised a litter and started again for the hospital. We soon reached the San Juan river which we forded with the water up to our shoulders. At the foot of El Paso hill we found Surgeon Church, who was our regimental surgeon, so we turned Carr over to him and started for our packs on the hill to find something to eat. We found very

little left but managed to scrape a little together that
the Cubans had left. We then started for the front
but the Colonel in command of the artillery said we
could not go then as he was about to open with his guns
and we would be exactly in range of the return fire.
We were about three miles to the rear and it was late
in the afternoon but still we could hear the roar of
the battle which showed no signs of abating. Thinking to get around the hill and reach the front before
it was dark, we started down the river road when
Harry, overcome by the heat, staggered and fell in my
arms. We soon brought him to, but he was very
weak and could not walk far but he told us to leave
him, and get to the front if we could. However, we
would not leave Harry with no one to care for him
so decided to bivouac for the niget where we were and
go to the front the next morning. Accordingly we
got some blankets and made camp for the night. As
we lay beside the road, the Thirty-Fourth Michigan
came along and I found a couple of fellows in one of
the companies who used to work for Wells-Higman
at Traverse City and knew my father well. On
account of sharpshooters we did not dare to build a
fire but turned in and had our first sleep in thirty-six
hours, with the stars shining in our eyes. We were
awakened several times by sharpshooters firing on us
but managed to get some sleep. In the morning
we were up before it was light and as Harry felt much
better we decided to start for the front as the battle
had already begun. Before starting I got some paper
and a pencil from Richard Harding Davis and wrote a
letter home.

SUNDAY, JULY 3RD.

We started at a brisk pace for we felt sure that
the finish was near and wanted to be back on the fir-

ing line again. I will never forget the sight we saw along the road. It was strewn with blankets, uniforms, canteens and other implements of war, while as we approached the front we saw wounded and dead men on every hand. Here was a gatling gun that had been burned out, while beside it lay three gunners cold in death; there a horse lay disembowled by a shell with the vultures and land craps already at work. As we crossed the river and started up the hill towards the block house, bullets began to fly by. They struck the trees overhead and the ground underfoot and cut holes in the air on every side. Wounded men continually passed us. It seemed hard that having paid their dues they should not be granted a respite, but the bullets pursued them cruelly all the way down the trail. The sight on the hill was terrible. Regulars, colored and white, mingled with Rough Riders, lay stiff and cold in their last, long sleep, some still holding their guns in their clenched fists. They were already bloated beyond recognition, and a fearful stench arose with the morning mists; but we hurry on continually passing wounded men going to the rear. We found our position about six o'clock and reported to Captain Heuston. The men were all surprised to see Byrnes and I for some thought we had been killed before coming off our Cassock post as they had not seen us since. I found Knox who I had not seen since we started in the charge. He had become mixed up with the Sixteenth Regulars and had fought with them for two days. We embraced each other like brothers, for each was fearful that the other had been killed.

Harry and I were put into the entrenchments which we found had been deepened and considerably extended. The fire was very heavy and we had to lie close. Through sitting bent double in the entrenchments, our limbs and backs were stiff and cramped and we were weakened by the tropical sun, but it seemed good to feel that we were out of danger, for unless a well aimed shell burst over the entrenchment we were safe. Food and water was scarce and a heavy rain added to our miserable condition.

About nine o'clock the fleet opened up. At first we thought that they were bombarding the city, but later we learned that Cervera's fleet had sailed out. A terrific fire was maintained for about an hour. We could see nothing because in the first place it was dangerous to raise our heads above the entrenchments, and in the second place a range of hills shut off our view of the sea. But we had full faith in Sampson and knew that he would give as good as he got.

About four o'clock the Spaniards raised a flag of truce and the fire was suspended. Although, fearing treachery, we still kept our men in the entrenchments. It was then we learned that Sampson had entirely destroyed the Spanish fleet without the loss of a ship. That made us feel good for we knew the spirit of the Spaniards would be broken by such a crushing defeat.

MONDAY, JULY 4TH.

We worked all night last night on a bomb proof which we dug in the hillside so our men could have some protection if the Spaniards bombarded us. I was never so tired in all my life as I am this morning. There was considerable heavy firing last night just off Morro Castle, and we learned this morning that the Spanish cruiser Reina Mercedes had been sunk by Sampson's fleet while trying to escape under cover of darkness.

INCIDENTS.

Our loss in the last three days' fighting has been tremendous; out of 12,000 men engaged 2,004 have been killed or wounded. Among the killed in my troop is poor Cashion, the youngest boy in the regiment. He was shot beside me on the afternoon of the first days' fighting. Miller is mortally wounded and Johnson, Meagher, Holmes, Wetmore, Crockett, Carr and Bailey are wounded, the regiment losing over a hundred men.

The Spanish sharpshooters are still very harrassing in our rear. They fire on Red Cross men and the wounded without compunction. They imitate the cry of the cuckoo and nights we can hear them in the tops of tall palms and in the swamps. Besides this they have nearly all their batteries masked and protected by a Red Cross flag. We can count seventeen Red Cross flags from our lines.

The Seventy-first New York was the only regiment to disgrace itself during the fight. They first refused to leave the bush and charge the hill, and on the morning of the 2nd when placed in support of a battery they fell back in a panic. Two of the companies however remained and deserve great credit.

The Second Massachusetts fought well with Lawton at El Caney but was withdrawn from the firing line on account of being armed with the old black powder guns which drew the enemies' fire.

Our dynamite gun has been very effective and during the bombardment which will doubtless soon take place, unless the city surrenders, it ought to do a great deal of damage.

CHAPTER VI.

The Siege and Bombardment of Santiago.

TUESDAY, JULY 5TH.

I was in the entrenchments all day to-day. We expected the flag of truce would be taken down about four o'clock, but another truce was declared. Rations are beginning to come up now and we have a troop mess. Water is still very scarce as it is a mile to the river and only one man can go back at a time. The water we get is not fit to wash in, but we are glad to get the scanty allowance we do. We have no shelter of any kind and are drenched every day by the heavy rains which begin about three and last till five. However, we have sent a detail back for the shelter tents and haversacks which we left at El Paso hill on the morning of the first day's fighting.

The men are completely worn out; very few of them have had over ten hours' sleep out of the last one hundred and twenty hours. We pushed our entrenchments forward last night and that kept us busy until dawn when we had to go into the entrenchments again. A man is lucky to be on outpost duty now, for if he is not he has to work all night on the entrenchments. Our tents came up this afternoon but the Cubans had stolen all the rations, so we received only empty haversacks. The Cubans can eat even if they cannot fight. Knox got half a tent and I got a poncho so we have some covering now.

Knox left for Siboney this morning in order to bring up our mail for which we are all very anxious.

General Toral has offered to surrender the city if we will let him march out and take to the mountains with his soldiers, but Shafter has demanded an unconditional surrender and has threatened to bombard the city if his demands are not granted. Last night we were called out twice under arms by false alarms. A surprise is evidently expected for no one is allowed to leave camp on any pretext. We are gaining in strength every day for new guns are constantly being planted and new troops are coming up.

About four o'clock Hobson and his brave sailors were exchanged and brought into our lines. As he crossed our lines all the regimental bands played and three cheers were given. Then we all crowded around to shake hands with the "hero of the Merrimac." Hobson is a fine appearing, modest young man and wears with easy grace the honor that clings to him.

This afternoon the Stars and Stripes were planted along our entrenchments. These are the first that I have seen displayed since landing and they look very pretty as they wave in the light breeze.

A new gatling gun and several mortars came up last night; the mortars are to be masked on our right near the First Regular Cavalry. Knox brought up the mail last night and then went to the hospital this morning. He seems completely used up. We certainly appreciate the mail which he brought up for it has been nearly two weeks since we have received any.

I was in the entrenchments again to-day,   In

fact every man spends eighteen out of twenty-four hours in the entrenchments now.

FRIDAY, JULY 8TH.

Last night I was called out of the entrenchments and worked on a redoubt until relieved about daylight. We filled gunny sacks with dirt and formed a breastwork of them. The redoubt is to be used by our Sharpshooters during the bombardment.

SATURDAY, JULY 9TH.

I worked on another redoubt last night about two hundred yards from the Spanish outposts. It was bright moonlight and we expected to be fired on every minute, but we were not disturbed. After being relieved from that duty I expected to get a little rest, but when I returned to camp I was put at work filling sacks which were to be used as a break in front of our bomb proof, as we have located a ten-inch gun which is trained on the hill.

A Spanish soldier who deserted last night came into our lines and gave us a good deal of valuable information concerning the location of the guns in the city, etc. He said that a good many Spaniards would desert if they were not afraid that we would kill them.

About nine o'clock this morning, General Toral offered to surrender the city if we would let him march his men out and go into the mountains. This would give us the city and big guns. However, we hope his terms will not be accepted for we have got him now where we can go right in and brand him, as one of the cowboys said.

SUNDAY, JULY 10TH.

After being in the entrenchments last night, I got leave of absence and took a good swim. It is the first time I have had my clothes off in three weeks and I feel like a new man. I also borrowed a razor and shaved my beard which was becoming quite long.

I now feel ready for the bombardment which begins at four o'clock. As Colonel Wood has been commissioned as Brigadier-General and put in command of the brigade, Roosevelt now has full command of the regiment.

We all feel gloomy to-day for we have just heard of the death of "Teddy" Miller, who died last night at Siboney from wounds received in our charge on San Juan on July first. Teddy was a fine fellow and a true soldier. His father, Lewis Miller, is the founder of the Chautauqua Assembly and he is a brother-in-law of Thomas Edison, the famous electrician. He graduated from Yale only last year and was practicing law in New York city when the war broke out.

I am on the Sharpshooters detail this afternoon and will be placed with twenty other men in the front rifle pit, where we are expected to keep the Spanish gunners away from their guns.

At four o'clock sharp the Spanish flag of truce went down, and it had scarcely fluttered to the ground when our dynamite guns opened, then the gatlings, rapid fire guns and mortors began to tear the air. The enemy responded weakly and contented themselves with cheering. At dusk the firing ceased, with a loss of but two men on our side. Our dynamite and rapid fire guns did splendid execution.

MONDAY, JULY 11TH.

At daybreak this morning our Artillery began hammering the Spanish entrenchments. I was relieved from the firing line about seven and returned just in time to see the First Illinois Infantry come up. They presented a fine sight, thirteen hundred strong, and all with bright new uniforms and clean flags. The Spaniards are more active to-day and we have suffered some loss from their shells. Our Artillery seems to fire in a half-hearted sort of way. About noon a white flag went up on the Spanish side and the bombardment was over.

We broke camp late this afternoon and marched around on the extreme right and went into camp on the El Caney road. We immediately threw up earthworks on a height commanding the city and threw out heavy pickets. Our position is between the First Cavalry, which is on our left, and the First Illinois, which is on our right. We can see the city and bay very plainly and have a fine position. About midnight a heavy thunder shower camp up and flooded our camp. During the storm our pickets began firing and we were called out. Later I was put out on picket and then relieved and put on a scouting detail, returning about dawn, after being fired on by a Spanish outpost.

TUESDAY, JULY 12TH.

About six o'clock I was put out on a cassock post by Lieutenant Goodrich. I was so near the Spanish entrenchments that I was compelled to lie down on the wet ground in order to conceal myself. To make matters worse, another heavy rain came up and I was drenched. About noon our entrenchments being completed, I was relieved and returned to camp, wet and covered with mud.

Shipp, an Oklahoma fellow who has been sick and has no tent, is sharing my tent with me. I am getting worried about Knox as I have not heard a word from him since he left camp, and I fear he has been sent to the yellow fever hospital. At best a sick man has no chance to recover, for they are compelled to lie on the damp ground and have no medicine but quinine and very little food. If Knox is in the hospital I fear there is little show for him, and yet I am unable to get leave of absence in order to look him up, for every man who is able to stand on his feet is needed at the front, for the regiment, and indeed the whole army, is sadly depleted by the fever and bullets. We have not half the men at the front that we started out with.

WEDNESDAY, JULY 13TH.

I was on a cassock post last night with Sergeant Moran. We formed a double post with the First Cavalry, the post being located directly between the two regiments.

After coming off post I left camp and securing a Cuban guide, I visited El Caney, the scene of Lawton's fight on the first of July. All the refugees of Santiago, some twenty thousand, are collected there. It was a pitiable sight to see them, many of them so weak from hunger that they could not stand. I never saw a more dreadful sight than these half naked men, women and children wasted away until they were mere skin and bones.

I crossed the river and visited the fort on top of the hill. It was built of stone, strongly loop holed, and has walls three feet thick. Capron's Artillery did little damage to it. If it had not been for Lawton's desperate charge, I do not think the hill would have been taken.

El Caney seems a typical Cuban village with its adobe houses and straggling streets. I entered several of the houses and saw a number of very beautiful Cuban Senoritas who were very friendly to me.

I soon disposed of the few hardtack I had brought for my lunch and then returned to camp. I was just in time to see General Miles and his staff ride up. "Dick" Alger, Harvard '99, and son of Secretary Alger, is on Miles' staff, but I did not have a chance to speak with him, although I should like to have found out how everything was coming on in the United States, for we have no idea how matters stand at home or how long the war is liable to last.

THURSDAY, JULY 14TH.

I was detailed in the entrenchments to-day and spent the entire day there. About noon there was considerable cheering all along the line and Lieutenant Goodrich informed us that the city had capitulated, but Colonel Roosevelt said that the report had not been confirmed and he did not want us to cheer.

FRIDAY, JULY 15TH,

Report of surrender was confirmed this morning. Twelve thousand troops under Linares and eight thousand in Holquin under General Pando are to lay down their arms and be shipped to Spain at the expense of the United States. It is further reported that our troops are under yellow fever quarantine for five days, and that if no fever breaks out by the end of the quarantine period we are to go to Porto Rico with General Wheeler. We are to boil all our drinking water and are not allowed to leave camp or talk with any Cubans. Towards evening we received some mail. I was lucky enough to draw three letters.

About three o'clock the French embassy passed in carriages on their return to the city. I was in the entrenchments from 12 p. m. until 1 a. m.

SATURDAY, JULY 16TH.

This is a red letter day in my army experience for we had oatmeal for breakfast this morning. To say it tasted fine would be expressing it mildly; it seemed as if I couldn't eat enough.

The terms of surrender are that the Spaniards march out with flags flying, then furl their flags and stack their arms. All officers are to retain their side arms. Foreign transports will take them to Spain.

SUNDAY, JULY 17TH.

Reveille was sounded this morning for the first time since our charge on San Juan. It seemed good to hear the old bugle again. Cubans on their return to the city are continually passing camp. It is a pitiable sight to see them struggling along, so weak from starvation that they can barely stand. As our camp is directly on the road between El Caney and Santiago, we are in full view of the hungry, starving multitude.

At 11:45 we were called out and stood " at attention " while Captain Capron's battery fired a salute of twenty-one guns to the American flag which was raised on the palace at high noon. During the ceremony the regimental bands played the "Star Spangled Banner " and " My Country, 'Tis of Thee." General Lawton's brigade went into the city to receive the surrendered arms and do provost duty.

At last, after seventeen days of fighting and waiting, the city is ours, but at what a fearful cost. As I glance down the line and see the many vacant places, I think of the comrades who are not present to exult in the reward of their bravery and my happiness gives way to sorrow. But Santiago now is an American city, and our Santiago campaign with its hardships and fighting is over. If the war does not end we will probably embark for Porto Rico in a few days, and we all hope that it will be our last campaign. Only twenty-two men reported for duty this morning. Our rations today consisted of beans, coffee, sugar and hardtack. I was on guard from 6 p. m, till 12.

MONDAY, JULY 18TH.

We broke camp at nine o'clock and marched down the old Santiago road to El Caney. It was fearfully hot and although the pace was slow, yet many men, weakened by duty in the entrenchments, fever and dysentery, fell out. From El Caney we turned south and camped at the head of the San Juan river, just at the foot of the hills in a lonely valley only some two miles from the bay, which can be seen glistening in the sunshine from the top of a neighboring hill. The entire second brigade, consisting of the First Regular Cavalry, the Tenth Regular (Colored) Cavalry and the Rough Riders, are in camp here, but so many of the men are sick that the brigade could hardly muster a full regiment. Our loss in the three days' fighting at San Juan is now reported at two thousand and five killed and wounded.

TUESDAY, JULY 19TH.

The day passed very quietly, the guard duty being very light and the men given every chance to rest, which they were glad to do after the arduous entrenchment work and the long march. During the day General Somers' brigade, consisting of the Ninth, Third and Sixth Cavalry regiments, went into camp just above us. Our only duties are to draw our rations, consisting of flour, coffee and bacon, and to "fall in" for morning roll call. The rest of the time is our own, but even the men who are not sick are too weak to do much. The hospitals are so full that it is impossible to gain admittance unless your temperature is above 103 degrees, and even there you get no care.

The troop mail to-day consisted of three letters, one of which I was fortunate enough to receive. The letter was dated June 29th, and has taken nearly a month to reach me.

By order of General Wheeler commanding the cavalry division, we are allowed to bathe in the creek every night.

WEDNESDAY, JULY 20TH.

Harry Holt returned to camp from the hospital to-day ; was glad to see him back. I can get no news whatever of Knox and fear he is in the Yellow Fever hospital.

General Wood, formerly our Colonel, has been appointed Governor of the Province of Santiago.

THURSDAY, JULY 21ST.

Charlie Bull, Harvard '98, returned to camp to-day, having been back to the United States for nearly a month nursing a bad case of inflamatory rheumatism. Captain Heuston is sick and as First Sergeant Palmer is also sick, Paul Hunter is acting First Sergeant. I got drenched while on guard in the rain this afternoon and came down with a high fever.

FRIDAY, JULY 22ND.

I was quite sick during the night but feel better this morning ; however, I am rather weak from a long-standing case of dysentery with which nearly all the men are troubled. Walter Cook got me some rice which tasted very good. At dinner we had our first issue of fresh beef, which tasted fine, although I did not feel like eating much.

SATURDAY, JULY 23RD.

I felt as bad as ever this morning and reported to the surgeon at the hospital, but as my fever was only up to 102½ he reported me for duty, which gave me some hopes although I could hardly stand. We had more fresh beef to-day, also bread and canned peaches, but I could not eat anything, as tempting as it looked.

As we are all in rags we were glad to have an opportunity to sign for some more clothing to-day. Over half the men in camp are sick and more are coming down every day ; every morning a number of new graves are made and those that escaped the bullets are falling victims to the fever. At this rate we will soon not have enough well men for guard duty as light as it is.

MONDAY, JULY 25TH.

Felt better to-day and wrote some letters ; also traded three hardtack to a Cuban for a machete after he had refused to sell it for five dollars.

TUESDAY, JULY 26TH.

Was put on guard to-day but got an easy post. The rains seem increasing instead of diminishing and the camp is becoming all cut up.

Received ten letters in the mail to-day and a number of home papers which were eagerly read by all the troop although a month old.

WEDNESDAY, JULY 27TH.

Was on old guard fatigue duty to-day. Had to carry fire wood about three miles for headquarters. Another mail came today in which I received five letters and some magazines from a thoughtful lady friend.

THURSDAY, JULY 28TH.

We receive fresh beef right along now, also bread made in Santiago. The creek is getting so polluted that we have to carry all drinking water a long way.

FRIDAY, JULY 29TH.

The following notice posted in the hospital this morning made us all jubilant over the prospect of returning home:

"GENERAL WHEELER:
  Make it known to the men as soon as possible that as soon as the fever abates and command is able to move it will be sent to Long Island, N. Y.
                                        SHAFTER."

SATURDAY, JULY 30TH.

Received a large mail to-day, also had issued us some Red Cross underwear and government shoes and shirts which are very acceptable. Our new uniforms have been received but have not been issued. New York papers dated the twenty-third were received to-day.

SUNDAY, JULY 31ST.

Every one able to walk was sent out after wood this morning, as it is becoming very scarce. We had to pack it about two miles over a very rough trail. Shipp, my tent mate, is very sick to-day with a high fever.

MONDAY, AUGUST 1ST.

Mail received this morning. Papers from home said we would be returned soon.

TUESDAY, AUGUST 2ND.

Received another mail this morning, also full rations of coffee and sugar. Instead of getting better the men seem to be getting worse, and it is evident that unless we move soon we will not be able to move at all. It seems strange that we should be kept here where we are drenched by daily rains and weakened by the hot weather when we would recuperate so fast back in the States where we would be free from rains and have cooler weather, and where our sick could get some sort of care.

WEDNESDAY, AUGUST 3RD.

Our new uniforms were issued today; they are very handsome in their yellow trimmings. I am so thin that a Number 2 suit is too large for me whereas when I enlisted I required a Number 3 suit.

Report comes today that the Surgeon General has ordered that we cannot be returned to the States in our present condition. Wood and Roosevelt have both sent letters and petitions asking that we be returned immediately.

Dr. Church told me today that if I wished to recover from the dysentery I will have to confine myself to a diet of oatmeal, milk and toast. His prescription is rather ironical as oatmeal and milk are not to be had at any price.

THURSDAY, AUGUST 4TH.

Our pay roll is being made out today. It is reported that we will be loaded on the transports as soon as they can be made ready. The heat is almost unbearable.

FRIDAY, AUGUST 5TH.

We signed the pay roll today and were notified that we would leave Sunday.

SATURDAY, AUGUST 6TH.

This morning the first brigade of our division broke camp and were loaded on board the cars and taken to Santiago.

At eight this morning we received our long looked
for marching orders.   Before leaving camp we were
ordered to put on our new uniforms and burn the old
ones; also our bedding was burned.   About 12 c'clock
we "fell in" and marched over to the railroad where
we were loaded in box cars.   On arriving in Santiago,
we were marched down to the wharf and loaded on the
Miami (transport No. 1).   Before we sailed we all
drew two months' pay and were allowed to go into the
city and buy supplies.   Muxlow and I started out
together but soon found out that provisions were very
scarce.   However we found some guava jelly and
cheese for which we paid an exorbitant price.   We
also took the opportunity to see the city which we
had fought for so long.   We found many interesting
sights in the city, many of the streets being entrenched,
and many of the buildings being torn by our shells.   In
the course of our wanderings we found a restaurant
and sat down to a table for the first time in two months.
When it grew dark we returned to the transport.

MONDAY, AUGUST 8TH.

As I sit on deck in the early morning light a
beautiful sight is stretched before me; to the north at
the foot of the mountain lies the city of Santiago,
while to the south stretches the bay covered with
transports and merchant vessels all flying the stars and
stripes.   The bay is long, narrow and hemmed in by
high mountains, capped by small block houses.   On
the sides and in the coves are palm trees and thatched
huts, which call to mind the historic quiet and lazi-
ness of the tropics.   On the left, towering above the
entrance of the harbor, is Morro Castle, suggestful of
the mediæval strongholds of the robber barons, the
waves beating at its base have worn away the stone so

that now they thunder into their caverns with a true
Rider Haggard rumbling.   It was very beautiful.

As we left our moorings and steamed slowly down
the bay, the Third Cavalry band struck up '"The Star
Spangled banner" and as we stood with bared heads
a mighty shout went up.

As we sailed down the bay, we could plainly see
the batteries on the shore, the sunken Merrimac and
the Reina Mercedes with her guns pointing skyward
as she lay on her side.   The cliffs on each side were
lined with formidable looking guns, but above them
floated the stars and stripes.

Our trip north was made under as pleasant conditions as a crowded, stuffy transport would allow.
The sea was calm and the fresh, cool, sea breezes gave
us new life and vigor.   As we steamed slowly north-
ward new strength came day by day.

On the 14th we sighted land off the Jersey coast
and the next morning we anchored off Montauk Point.
Not until then did we learn that the Peace Protocol
had been signed and that hostilities had ceased.   But
in the midst of our rejoicing over this good news, we
were saddened by learning that Stanley Hollister had
died from the wounds received at San Juan, and that
William Saunders had died of fever on the hospital
ship.

After being inspected by quarantine officers, we
landed and marched to the "detention camp."   After
four days in the "detention camp" with no signs of
"yellow fever" we went across Long Island to our per-
manent quarters, where we got good food and comfort-
able tents.

On the 19th I received a ten days' furlough and
as I already felt the chills and fever coming on I hast-
ened to New York City where I was joined by my
mother, father and sister.   As I received my dis-